"Three Christmas

A Cat's Tal

by Gill Valentine

Merry Xmas
2015

To Lizzy
love from
Gill Valentine

ISBN: 978-1-326-49688-3

PublishNation
www.publishnation.co.uk

This book is dedicated to Leila who loved Christmas time, kittens and cats.

It was a snowy crisp evening, in fact a Christmas Eve.

Three little kittens sat quietly in a field.

They gazed in awe at a desert of white.

Shivering and wondering what happened to make everything so bright.

The sun shone down as it set far away.

Then suddenly, what on earth was this?

Could it be…………………?

It was Santa on his sleigh!

His reindeer before him, flying high in the sky.

The three little kittens just stared
up above.

They were quite amazed to see
such a vision fly by.

My goodness I do hope that
Santa comes to me.

They all thought the same as they
looked at him with glee.

The presents they wished for included cat toys, a ball of wool or a fluffy little mouse.

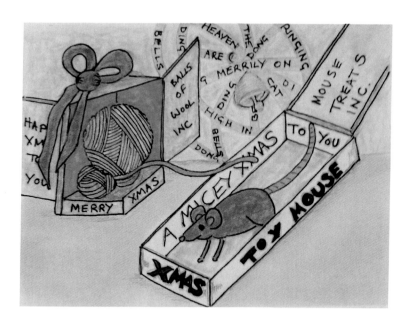

With his reindeers in front he steered his sleigh at the fastest of speeds.

Santa disappeared as quickly as he came in such a flash.

Now bright stars glistened across
the snowy night-time sky.

Some moments passed by and
the kittens just wondered why.

They could not believe just what
they had seen flying by.

They looked at each other now that Santa had gone, as they tried to remember just what was for tea.

Maybe it would be a lovely roast bird, a morsel of cheese or salmon for a treat.

They hoped that their fish dish would be full to the brim with yummy things to eat.

They quickly ran home to tell their snowy tale and hoped they would see Santa again another day.

They finished their lovely tea and drank up all their milk.

Then hurried straight upstairs to bed with smiles upon each face.

They hung their Christmas
stockings around their cosy bed.

They tried and tried to go to
sleep. They wriggled and
wriggled around in bed but they
just could not settle their sleepy
little heads.

They felt so excited with
butterflies in their tummies they
thought they might just burst.

Early next morning when they
woke up, they ran down the
stairs so fast they almost flew.

They wanted so much to see
what was under the big green
Christmas Tree.

They found all the presents they
had wished as they jumped up
and down with glee.

Paws for
thought……………………………………..

A very merry Christmas to all
human beings from each little
kitten around the world.

Remember dear humans to
always be kind to all creatures no
matter how big or small.

Do not forget that it is very
important to be kind to other
humans too.

Especially if you want Santa to come and see you........

THE END